Diamond and the North Wind

For my family.

Thank you Anna Marie and my other dear friends who have encouraged me throughout this process.

Diamond and the North Wind

ISBN: 978-1-54394-996-4

Artwork was done in graphite and watercolor, and finalized in Photoshop.

Diamond and the North Wind

By George MacDonald ♦ Illustrated by Juliette Watts

Adapted from *At the Back of the North Wind*

by George MacDonald ©1871

I have been asked to tell you about the North Wind. An old Greek writer mentions a people who lived at the North Wind's back. My story does not begin the same way. I am going to tell you about a boy who met North Wind and how it fared with him.

He lived in a low room over a coach house. This room was always cold, except in summer, when the sun took the matter into his own hands. Indeed, I am not sure whether I ought to call it a room at all, for it was just a loft where they kept hay and straw and oats for the horses. And when little Diamond—but stop: I must tell you that his father, who was a coachman, had named him after a favorite horse, and his mother had no objection. When little Diamond, then, lay there in bed, he could hear the horses under him munching away in the dark, or moving sleepily in their dreams. For Diamond's father had built him a bed in the loft with boards all round it, because they had so little room in their own end over the coach house; and Diamond's father put old Diamond in the stall under the bed, because he was a quiet horse, and did not go to sleep standing, but lay down like a reasonable creature. And although old Diamond was very quiet all night long, yet when he woke he got up like an earthquake, and then young Diamond knew what time it was, or at least what was to be done next, which was to go to sleep again as fast as he could.

There was hay at his feet and hay at his head, piled up in great trusses to the very roof. Indeed it was sometimes only through a little lane with several turnings that he could reach his bed at all. For the stock of hay was, of course, always in a state either of slow ebb or of sudden flow. Sometimes the whole space of the loft, with the little panes in the roof for the stars to look in, would lie open before his eyes as he lay in bed; sometimes a yellow wall of sweet-smelling fibers closed up his view at the distance of half a yard. He had not the least idea that the wind got in at a chink in the wall, and blew about him all night. For the back of his bed was only of boards an inch thick, and on the other side of them was the north wind.

Now, as I have already said, these boards were soft and crumbly. Hence it happened that little Diamond found one night, after he lay down, that a knot had come out of one of them, and that the wind was blowing in upon him in a cold and rather imperious fashion. So he jumped out of bed, got a little strike of hay, twisted and folded it, and, having made it into a cork, stuck it into the hole in the wall. But the wind began to blow loud and angrily, and, as Diamond was falling asleep, out blew his cork and hit him on the nose, just hard enough to wake him up quite, and let him hear the wind whistling shrill in the hole. It popped out again several more times before he gave up, drew the blankets over his head, and was soon fast asleep.

Although the next day was very stormy, Diamond forgot all about the hole. His mother, however, discovered it, and pasted a bit of brown paper over it, so that, when Diamond had snuggled down the next night, he had no occasion to think of it.

Presently, however, he lifted his head and listened.

Who could that be talking to him? The wind was rising again, and getting very loud, and full of rushes and whistles. He was sure someone was talking, and very near him, too. But he was not frightened, for he had not yet learned how to be. So he sat up and listened. The voice appeared to come from the back of the bed. He crept nearer to it, and laid his ear over the hole, and then he heard the voice quite distinctly. There was, in fact, a little corner of the paper loose, and through that, as from a mouth in the wall, the voice came.

"What do you mean, little boy, closing up my window?"

"What window?" asked Diamond.

"You stuffed hay into it three times last night. I had to blow it out again three times."

"You can't mean this little hole! It isn't a window, it's a hole in my bed."

"I did not say it was a window. I said it was my window."

"But it can't be a window, because windows are holes to see out of."

"Well, that's just what I made this window for."

"But you are outside: you can't want a window."

"You are quite mistaken. Windows are to see out of, you say. Well, I'm in my house, and I want windows to see out of it."

"But you've made a window into my bed."

"Well, your mother has got three windows into my dancing room, and you have three into my garret."

"But I heard father say, when my mother wanted him to make a window through the wall, that it was against the law, for it would look into Mr. Dyves's garden."

The voice laughed.

"The law would have some trouble to catch me!" it said.

"But if it's not right, you know," said Diamond, "that's no matter. You shouldn't do it."

"I am so tall I am above that law," said the voice.

"You must have a tall house, then," said Diamond.

"Yes; a tall house: the clouds are inside it."

Diamond thought a minute. "I think, then, you can hardly expect me to keep a window in my bed for you. Why don't you make a window into Mr. Dyves's bed?"

"Nobody makes a window into an ash pit," said the voice, rather sadly. "I like to see nice things out of my windows."

"But he must have a nicer bed than I have, though mine is very nice, so nice that I couldn't wish a better."

"It's not the bed I care about: it's what is in it. But you just open that window."

"Well, mother says I shouldn't be disobliging; but it's rather hard. You see the north wind will blow right in my face if I do."

"I am the North Wind."

"Oh!" said Diamond, thoughtfully. "Then will you promise not to blow on my face if I open your window?"

"I can't promise that. But I do promise that you shall not be the worse for it. You will be much the better for it. Just believe what I say, and do as I tell you."

"Well, I can pull the blankets over my head," said Diamond, and feeling with his little sharp nails, he got hold of the open edge of the paper and tore it off at once.

In came a long whistling spear of cold, and struck his little chest. He scrambled and tumbled in under the bedclothes, and covered himself up. There was no paper now between him and the voice, and he felt a little, not frightened exactly—he had not learned that yet—but rather queer; for what a strange person this North Wind must be that lived in the great house "called Out-of-Doors, I suppose," thought Diamond, and made windows into people's beds! But the voice began again, and he could hear it quite plainly, even with his head under the bed clothes. It was a still more gentle voice now, although six times as large and loud as it had been, and he thought it sounded a little like his mother's.

"What is your name, little boy?" it asked.

"Diamond," answered Diamond, under the bed clothes.

"What a funny name!"

"It's a very nice name," returned its owner. Diamond is a great and good horse, and he sleeps right under me. He is old Diamond, and I am young Diamond.

Or, if you like it better, for you're very particular, Mr. North Wind, he's big Diamond, and I'm little Diamond."

A beautiful laugh, large but very soft and musical, sounded somewhere beside him, but Diamond kept his head under the blankets.

"I'm not Mr. North Wind," said the voice.

"You told me that you were the North Wind," insisted Diamond.

"I did not say Mister North Wind," said the voice.

"Well, then, I do; for mother tells me I ought to be polite."

"Then let me tell you I don't think it at all polite of you to say Mister to me."

"Well, I didn't know better. I'm very sorry."

You can't say it's polite to lie there talking with your head under the bed clothes, and never look up to see what kind of person you are talking to. I want you to come outside with me."

"I want to go to sleep," said Diamond, vexed.

"You shall sleep all the better tomorrow night."

"Besides," said Diamond, "you are out in the garden next door, and I can't get there. I can only get into our own yard."

"Will you take your head out of the bed clothes?" said the voice, just a little angrily.

"No!" answered Diamond, half peevish, half frightened.

The instant he said the word, a tremendous blast of wind crashed in a board of the wall, and swept the blankets off Diamond. He started up in terror. Leaning over him was the large, beautiful, pale face of a woman. Her dark eyes looked a little angry, for they had just begun to flash; but a quivering in her sweet upper lip made her look as if she were going to cry. What was the most strange was that away from her head streamed out her black hair in every direction, so that the darkness in the hayloft looked as if it were made of her. But as Diamond gazed at her, entranced with her mighty beauty, her hair began to gather itself out of the darkness, and fell down all about her again, till her face looked out of the midst of it like a moon out of a cloud. From her eyes came all the light by which Diamond saw her face and her hair; and that was all he did see of her yet. The wind was over and gone.

"Will you go with me now, you little Diamond? I am sorry I was forced to be so rough with you," said the lady.

"I will. Yes, I will," answered Diamond, holding out both his arms. "But," he added, dropping them, "how shall I get my clothes? They are in mother's room, and the door is locked."

"Oh, never mind your clothes. You will not be cold. I shall take care of that. Nobody is cold with the north wind."

"I thought everybody was," said Diamond.

"That is a great mistake. Most people make it, however. They are cold because they are not with the north wind, but without it."

If Diamond had been a little older, and had supposed himself a good deal wiser, he would have thought the lady was joking. But he was not older, and did not fancy himself wiser, and therefore understood her well enough. Again he stretched out his arms. The lady's face drew back a little.

"Follow me, Diamond," she said.

"Yes," said Diamond, only a little ruefully.

You're not afraid?" said the North Wind.

"No, ma'am; but mother never lets me go out without shoes. She never said anything about clothes, so I guess she wouldn't mind that."

"I know your mother very well," said the lady. "She is a good woman. I have visited her often. I was with her when you were born. I saw her laugh and cry both at once. I love your mother, Diamond. And I know all about you and your mother."

"Yes. I will go with you."

"Now for the next question: you're not to call me ma'am. You must call me just my own name—respectfully, you know—just North Wind."

"Well, please, North Wind, you are so beautiful, I am quite ready to go with you."

"You must not be ready to go with everything beautiful all at once, Diamond."

"But what's beautiful can't be bad. You're not bad, North Wind?"

"No, I'm not bad. But sometimes beautiful things grow bad by doing bad, and it takes some time for their badness to spoil their beauty. So little boys may be mistaken if they go after things because they are beautiful."

"Well, I will go with you because you are beautiful and good, too."

"Ah, but there's another thing, Diamond: What if I should look ugly without being bad—look ugly myself because I am making ugly things beautiful? What then?"

"I don't quite understand you, North Wind. You tell me. What then?"

"Well, if you see me with my face all black, don't be frightened. If you see me flapping wings like a bat's, as big as the whole sky, don't be frightened. If you hear me raging ten times worse than Mrs. Bill, the blacksmith's wife, even if you see me looking in at people's windows like Mrs. Eve Dropper, the gardener's wife, you must believe that I am doing my work. Nay, Diamond, if I change into a serpent or a tiger, you must not let go your hold of me, for my hand will never change in yours if you keep a good hold. If you keep a hold, you will know who I am all the time, even when you look at me and can't see me the least like the North Wind. I may look something very awful. Do you understand?"

"Quite well," said little Diamond.

"Come along, then," said North Wind, and disappeared behind the mountain of hay.

Diamond crept out of bed and followed her.

When Diamond got round the corner of the hay, for a moment he hesitated. The stair by which he would naturally have gone down to the door was at the other side of the loft, and looked very black indeed; for it was full of North Wind's hair, as she descended before him. And just beside him was the ladder going straight down into the stable. Through the opening in the floor the faint gleam of the stable lantern was enticing, and Diamond thought he would run down that way.

The stair went close past the loose-box in which Diamond the horse lived. When Diamond the boy was half way down, he remembered that it was no use going this way, for the stable door was locked. But at the same moment there was horse Diamond's great head poked out of his box on to the ladder, for he knew boy Diamond although he was in his nightshirt, and wanted him to pull his ears for him. This Diamond did very gently for a minute or so, and patted and stroked his neck too, and kissed the big horse, and had begun to take the bits of straw and hay out of his mane, when all at once he remembered that the Lady North Wind was waiting for him in the yard.

"Good night, Diamond," he said, and darted up the ladder, across the loft, and down the stair to the door. But when he got out into the yard, there was no lady.

Now it is always a dreadful thing to think there is somebody and find nobody. Children in particular have not made up their minds to it; they generally cry at nobody, especially when they wake up at night. But it was an especial disappointment to Diamond, for his little heart had been beating with joy: the face of the North Wind was so grand! To have a lady like that for a friend, with such long hair, too! Why, it was longer than twenty Diamonds' tails! She was gone. And there he stood, with his bare feet on the stones of the paved yard.

It was a clear night overhead, and the stars were shining. Diamond, however, had not been out so late before in all his life, and things looked so strange about him!—just as if he had got into Fairyland, of which he knew quite as much as anybody. For his mother had no money to buy books to set him wrong on the subject. I have seen this world—only sometimes, just now and then, you know—look as strange as ever I saw Fairyland. But I confess that I have not yet seen Fairyland at its best. I am always going to see it so some time.

But if you had been out in the face and not at the back of the North Wind on a cold rather frosty night, and in your nightshirt, it would have felt quite as strange to you as it did to Diamond. He cried a little, just a little, he was so disappointed to lose the lady.

But it can't be denied that a little gentle crying does one good. It did Diamond good; for as soon as it was over he was a brave boy again.

"She won't say it was my fault, anyhow!" said Diamond. "I bet she is hiding somewhere to see what I will do. I'll look for her."

So he went around the stable towards the kitchen garden. But the moment he was clear of the shelter of the stable, sharp as a knife came the wind against his little chest and his bare legs. He tried to go on, but when he got past the weeping ash that stood in the corner, the wind blew much stronger, and it grew stronger and stronger till he could hardly fight against it. And it was so cold! All the flashy spikes of the stars seemed to have got somehow into the wind.

Then he thought of what the lady had said about people being cold because they were not with the North Wind. How it was that he should have guessed what she meant at that very moment I cannot tell, but I have observed that the most wonderful thing in the world is how people come to understand anything. He turned his back to the wind, and trotted again towards the yard. Strange to say, it blew so much more gently against his calves than it had blown against his shins that he began to feel almost warm by contrast.

You must not think it was cowardly of Diamond to turn his back to the wind: he did so only because he thought Lady North Wind had told him something like this. If she had said to him that he must hold his face to it, Diamond would have held his face to it. But the most foolish thing is to fight for no good, and to please nobody.

Well, it was just as if the wind was pushing Diamond along. If he turned round, it grew very sharp especially on his legs, and so he thought it might really be Lady North Wind, though he could not see her, and he had better let her blow him wherever she pleased. So she blew and blew, and he went and went, until he found himself standing at a door in a wall, which door led from the yard into a little belt of shrubbery, flanking Mr. Coleman's house. Mr. Coleman was his father's master, and the owner of Diamond.

He opened the door, and went through the shrubbery, and out into the middle of the lawn, still hoping to find North Wind. The soft grass was very pleasant to his bare feet, and felt warm after the stones of the yard, but the lady was nowhere to be seen. Then he began to think that after all he must have done wrong, and she was offended with him for not following close after her, but staying to talk to the horse.

There he stood in the middle of the lawn, the wind blowing his nightshirt till it flapped like a loose sail. The stars were very shiny over his head; but they did not give light enough to show that the grass was green, and Diamond stood alone in the strange night, which looked half solid all about him. He began to wonder whether he was in a dream or not. It was important to determine this; "for," thought Diamond, "if I am in a dream, I am safe in my bed, and I needn't cry. But if I'm not in a dream, I'm out here, and perhaps I had better cry, and besides, I'm not sure I can help it." He came to the conclusion, however, that, whether he was in a dream or not, there could be no harm in not crying for a little while longer: he could begin whenever he liked.

The back of Mr. Coleman's house was to the lawn, and one of the drawing room windows looked out upon it. The ladies had not gone to bed, for the light was still shining in that window. But they had no idea that a little boy was standing on the lawn in his nightshirt, or they would have run out in a moment. And as long as he saw that light, Diamond could not feel quite lonely. He stood staring, not at the great warrior Orion in the sky, nor yet at the disconsolate, neglected moon going down in the west, but at the drawing room window with the light shining through its curtains. He had been in that room once or twice that he could remember at Christmas times, for the Colemans were kind people, though they did not care much about children.

All at once it went nearly out: he could only see a glimmer of the shape of the window. Then, indeed, he felt that he was left alone. It was so dreadful to be out in the night after everybody was gone to bed! That was more than he could bear. He burst out crying in good earnest, beginning with a wail like that of the wind when it is waking up.

Perhaps you think this was very foolish. Could he not go home to his own bed again when he liked? Yes, but it looked dreadful to him to creep up that stair again and lie down in his bed, knowing that North Wind's window was open beside him, and he might never see her again. He would be just as lonely there as here. Nay, it would be much worse if he had to think that the window was nothing but a hole in the wall.

At the very moment when he burst out crying, the old nurse came to the back door, which was of glass, to close the shutters. She thought she heard a cry, and, peering out, she saw something white on the lawn. Too old and too wise to be frightened, she opened the door, and went straight towards the white thing to see what it was. And when Diamond saw her coming he was not frightened either, though Mrs. Crump was a little cross sometimes; for there is a good kind of crossness that is only disagreeable, and there is a bad kind of

crossness that is very nasty indeed. So she came, peering into the night. When she saw Diamond, she made a great exclamation, and threw up her hands. Then without a word, for she thought Diamond was walking in his sleep, she caught hold of him, and led him towards the house.

He made no objection, for he was just in the mood to be grateful for notice of any sort, and Mrs. Crump led him straight into the drawing room.

Miss Coleman was brushing her hair by the drawing room fire. The young lady was very lovely, though not nearly so beautiful as North Wind; her hair was extremely long, for it came down to her knees, though that was nothing at all to North Wind's hair. Yet when she looked round, with her hair all about her, as Diamond entered, he thought for one moment that it was North Wind, and, pulling his hand from Mrs. Crump's, he stretched out his arms and ran towards Miss Coleman. He saw the next moment that she was not Lady North Wind, but she looked so like her he could not help running into her arms and bursting into tears afresh.

Mrs. Crump said the poor child had walked out in his sleep, and Diamond thought she ought to know, and did not contradict her. For anything he knew, it might be so indeed. He let them talk on about him, and said nothing. And when, after their astonishment was over and Miss Coleman had given him a sponge cake, it was decreed that Mrs. Crump should take him to his mother, he was quite satisfied.

His mother had to get out of bed to open the door when Mrs. Crump knocked. She was indeed surprised to see her boy, and having taken him in her arms and carried him to his bed, returned and had a long confabulation with Mrs. Crump, for they were still talking when Diamond fell fast asleep, and could hear them no longer.

Diamond woke very early in the morning, and thought what a curious dream he had had. But the memory grew brighter and brighter in his head, until it did not look altogether like a dream, and he began to think that perhaps he really had been abroad in the wind last night. He decided that if he had been brought home to his mother by Mrs. Crump, she would say something to him about it, and that would settle the matter. Then he got up and dressed himself, but, finding that his father and mother were not yet stirring, he went

down the ladder to the stable. There he found that even old Diamond was not awake yet, for he was lying as flat as a horse could lie upon his nice trim bed of straw.

I'll give old Diamond a surprise, thought the boy, and creeping up softly, before the horse knew it, he was upon his back. Then it was Diamond's turn to have a surprise because as with an earthquake, a rumbling and rocking, and a sprawling of legs and heaving of backs, young Diamond found himself up in the air with both hands twisted in the horse's mane. Then the horse stood as still as a stone, for he knew that it was young Diamond upon his back, and he was a good boy, and old Diamond was a good horse, and the one was all right on the back of the other.

During this time his mother woke, and her first thought was to see her boy. She had visited him twice during the night, and found him sleeping quietly. Now his bed was empty, and she was frightened.

"Diamond! Diamond! Where are you, Diamond?" she called out.

Diamond turned his head where he sat like a knight on his steed in enchanted stall, and cried aloud,

"Here, mother, on Diamond's back."

She came running to the ladder, and peeping down, saw him aloft on the great horse.

"Get down, Diamond," she said.

"I can't," answered Diamond.

"How did you get up?" asked his mother.

"Quite easily," answered he; "but when I got up, Diamond got up too, and so here I am."

His mother thought he had been walking in his sleep again, and hurried down the ladder. She did not much like going up to the horse, for she was frightened of horses, but she would have gone into a lion's den, not to say a horse's stall, to help her boy. So she went and lifted him off Diamond's back, and felt braver all her life after this. She carried him in her arms up to her room, but, afraid of frightening him at his own sleep walking, as she supposed it, said nothing about last night. Before the next day was over, Diamond had almost concluded the whole adventure was a dream.

For a week his mother watched him very carefully, going into the loft several times a night, as often, in fact, as she woke. Every time she found him fast asleep.

All that week it was hard weather. The grass showed white in the morning with the hoar-frost which clung like tiny comfits to every blade. And as Diamond's shoes were not good, and his mother had not quite saved up enough money to get him the new pair she so much wanted for him, she would not let him run out. He played all his games over and over indoors.

At length his mother brought home his new shoes, and no sooner did she find they fitted him than she told him he might run out in the yard and amuse himself for an hour.

The sun was going down when he flew from the door like a bird from its cage. All the world was new to him. A great fire of sunset burned on the top of the gate that led from the stables to the house; above the fire in the sky lay a large lake of green light, above that a golden cloud, and over that the blue of the wintry heavens. And Diamond thought that, next to his own home, he had never seen any place he would like so much to live in as that sky. For it is not fine things that make home a nice place, but your mother and your father.

As he was looking at the lovely colours, the gates were thrown open, and there was old Diamond and his friend leading the carriage, dancing with impatience to get at their stalls and their oats. And in they came. Diamond was not in the least afraid of his father driving over him, but, careful not to spoil the grand show he made with his fine horses and his multitudinous cape, with a red edge to every fold, he slipped out of the way and let him dash right on to the stables. To be quite safe he had to step into the recess of the door that led from the yard to the shrubbery.

As he stood there he remembered how the wind had driven him to this same spot on the night of his dream. And once more he was almost sure that it was no dream.

At length he ran to the stable to see his father make Diamond's bed. Then his father took him in his arms, carried him up the ladder, and set him down at the table where they were going to have their tea.

It was bed time soon, and Diamond went to bed and fell fast asleep.

He awoke all at once, in the dark.

"Open the window, Diamond," said a voice.

Now Diamond's mother had once more pasted up North Wind's window.

"Are you North Wind?" asked Diamond. "I don't hear you blowing."

"No. But you hear me talking. Open the window, for I don't have much time."

Diamond scratched at the paper like ten mice, and getting hold of the edge of it, tore it off. The next instant a young girl glided across the bed, and stood upon the floor.

"Oh dear!" said Diamond, quite dismayed; "I didn't know. Who are you, please?"

"I'm North Wind."

"Are you really?"

"Yes. "Hurry, then, if you want to go with me."

"But you are not big enough to take care of me. I think you are only Miss North Wind."

"I am big enough to show you the way, anyhow. I'm not in such a hurry as I was the other night. Dress as fast as you can, and I'll go and shake the primrose leaves till you come."

Springing out of bed, Diamond dressed himself as fast as ever he could. Then he crept out into the yard, through the door in the wall, and away to the primrose. Behind it stood North Wind, leaning over it, and looking at the flower as if she had been its mother. "Come along," she said, jumping up and holding out her hand.

Diamond took her hand. It was cold, but so pleasant and full of life, it was better than warm. She led him across the garden. With one bound she was on the top of the wall. Diamond was left on the ground. She reached down, Diamond took hold of her hand, gave a great spring, and stood beside her.

"This is nice!" he said.

Another bound, and they stood in the road by the river. It was full tide, and the stars were shining clear in its depths, for it lay still, waiting for its turn to run down again to the sea. They walked along its side. But they had not walked far before its surface was covered with ripples, and the star reflections had vanished.

North Wind was now tall as a full-grown girl. Her hair was flying about her head, and the wind was blowing a breeze down the river. But she turned aside and went up a narrow lane, and as she went her hair fell down around her.

"I have some rather disagreeable work to do tonight," she said, "before I get out to sea, and I must get started at once. The disagreeable work must be done first."

So saying, she laid hold of Diamond and began to run, gliding along faster and faster. Diamond kept up with her as well as he could. Once they ran through a hall where they found back and front doors open. At the foot of the stair North Wind stood still, and Diamond, hearing a great growl, started in terror, and there, instead of North Wind, was a huge wolf by his side. He let go his hold in fear, and the wolf bounded up the stair. The windows of the house rattled and shook as if guns were firing, and the sound of a great fall came from above. Diamond stood with white face staring up at the landing.

"Surely," he thought, "North Wind can't be eating one of the children!" Coming to himself all at once, he rushed after her with his little fist clenched. There were ladies in long trains going up and down the stairs, and gentlemen in white neckties attending on them, who stared at him, but none of them were of the people of the house, and they said nothing. Before he reached the head of the stair, however, North Wind met him, took him by the hand, and hurried down and out of the house.

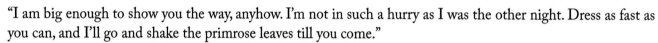

"I hope you haven't eaten a baby, North Wind!" said Diamond, very solemnly.

North Wind laughed merrily, and went tripping on faster. Her grassy robe swept and swirled about her steps, and wherever it passed over withered leaves, they went fleeing and whirling in spirals, and running on their edges like wheels, all about her feet.

"No," she said at last, "I did not eat a baby. You would not have had to ask that question if you had not let go of my hand. You would have seen how I served a nurse that was calling a child bad names, and telling her she was wicked. She had been drinking. I saw an ugly gin bottle in a cupboard."

"And you frightened her?" said Diamond.

"I believe so!" answered North Wind laughing merrily. "I flew at her throat, and she tumbled over on the floor with such a crash that they ran in. She'll be turned away tomorrow, and quite time, if they knew as much as I do."

"But didn't you frighten the little one?"

"She never saw me. The woman would not have seen me either if she had not been wicked."

"Oh!" said Diamond, dubiously.

"Why should you see things," returned North Wind, "that you wouldn't understand or know what to do with? Good people see good things; bad people see bad things."

"Then are you a bad thing?"

"No. For you see me, Diamond, dear," said the girl, and she looked down at him, and Diamond saw the loving eyes of the great lady beaming from the depths of her falling hair.

"I had to make myself look like a bad thing before she could see me. If I had put on any other shape than a wolf's she would not have seen me, for that is what is growing to be her own shape inside of her."

They were now climbing the slope of a grassy ascent. It was Primrose Hill, in fact, although Diamond had never heard of it.

The moment they reached the top, North Wind stood and turned her face towards London. The stars were still shining clear and cold overhead. There was not a cloud to be seen. The air was sharp, but Diamond did not find it cold.

"Now," said the lady, "whatever you do, do not let my hand go. I might have lost you the last time, only I was not in a hurry then: now I am in a hurry."

Yet she stood still for a moment.

And as she stood looking towards London, Diamond saw that she was trembling.

"Are you cold, North Wind?"

"No, Diamond," she answered, looking down upon him with a smile. "I am only getting ready to sweep one of my rooms. Those careless, greedy, untidy children make it in such a mess."

As she spoke he could have told by her voice, if he had not seen with his eyes, that she was growing larger and larger. Her head went up and up towards the stars; and as she grew, still trembling through all her body, her hair also grew longer and longer, lifted itself from her head, and went out in black waves. The next moment, however, it fell back around her, and she grew less and less till she was only a tall woman. Then she put her hands behind her head, and gathered some of her hair, and began weaving and knotting it together. When she had done, she bent down her beautiful face close to his, and said "Diamond, I am afraid you would not keep hold of me, and if I were to drop you, I don't know what might happen; so I have been making a place for you in my hair. Come. Get in, Diamond."

And Diamond parted her hair with his hands, crept between, and feeling about soon found the woven nest. It was just like a pocket. North Wind put her hands to her back, felt all about the nest, and finding it safe, said, "Are you comfortable, Diamond?"

"Yes, very," answered Diamond.

The next moment he was rising in the air. North Wind grew towering up to the place of the clouds. Her hair went streaming out away from her, till it spread like a mist over the stars. She flung herself out into space.

Diamond held on by two of the twisted ropes. As soon as he had come to himself, he peeped through the woven shelter. The earth was rushing past like a river or a sea below him. Trees, water, and green grass hurried away beneath.

And now there was nothing but the roofs of houses, sweeping along like a great torrent of stones and rocks.

Chimney pots fell, and tiles flew from the roofs. There was a great roaring, for the wind was dashing against London like a sea. But at North Wind's back Diamond, of course, felt nothing of it all. He was in a perfect calm. He could only hear the sound of it.

Soon he raised himself and looked over the edge of his nest. There were the houses rushing up and shooting away below him, like a fierce torrent of rocks instead of water. Then he looked up to the sky, but could see no stars; they were hidden by the blinding masses of the lady's hair which swept between. He began to wonder whether she would hear him if he spoke. He would try.

"Please, North Wind," he said, "what is that noise?"

From high over his head came the voice of North Wind, answering him, gently, "The noise of my broom. I am the old woman that sweeps the cobwebs from the sky; only I'm busy with the floor now."

"What makes the houses look as if they were running away?"

"I am sweeping so fast over them."

"North Wind, I knew London was very big, but I didn't know it was as big as this. It seems like we will never get away from it."

"We are going round and round, otherwise we would have left it long ago."

"Is this the way you sweep, North Wind?"

"Yes; I go round and round with my great broom."

"Please, would you mind going a little slower, for I want to see the streets?"

"You won't see much now."

"Why?"

"Because I have nearly swept all the people home."

"Oh! I forgot," said Diamond, and was quiet after that, for he did not want to be troublesome.

But she dropped a little towards the roofs of the houses, and Diamond could see down into the streets. There were very few people about, though. The lamps flickered and flared again, but nobody seemed to want them.

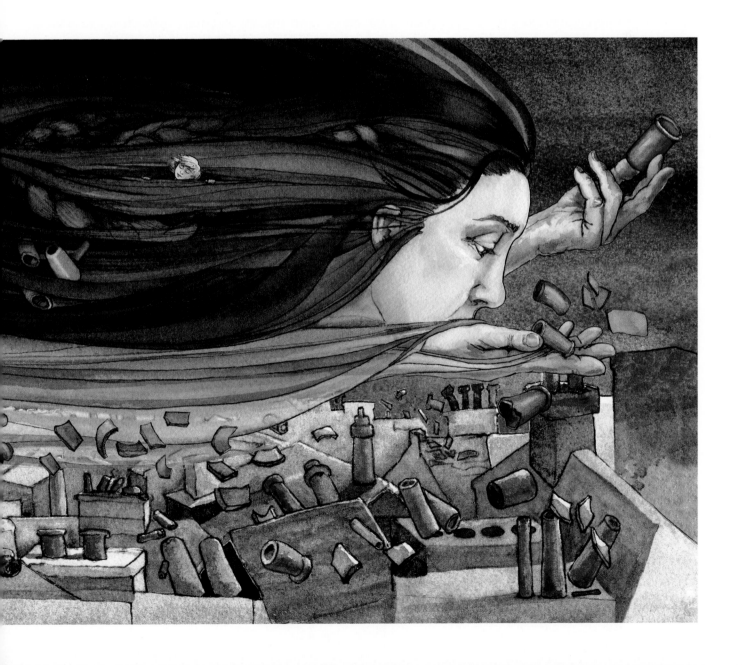

Suddenly Diamond spied a little girl coming along a street. She was dreadfully blown by the wind, and a broom she was trailing behind her was very troublesome. It seemed as if the wind kept after her like a wild beast, tearing at her rags. She was so lonely there!

"Oh, please, North Wind," he cried, "won't you help that little girl?"

"No, Diamond. I mustn't leave my work."

"But you're kind to me, dear North Wind. Why shouldn't you be as kind to her as you are to me?"

"There are reasons, Diamond. Everybody can't be dealt with the same way. Everybody is not ready for the same thing."

"But I don't see why I should be treated more kindly than she."

"Do you think nothing's to be done except what you can see, Diamond? It's all right. Of course you can help her if you like. You've got nothing particular to do at this moment. I have."

"Oh, do let me help her, then. But you won't be able to wait?"

"No, I can't wait; you must do it yourself. And, mind, the wind will get a hold of you, too."

"Don't you want me to help her, North Wind?"

"Not without having some idea what will happen. If you break down and cry, that won't be much of a help to her, and it will make a goose of little Diamond."

"I want to go," said Diamond. "Only there's just one thing: how am I to get home?"

"If you're anxious about that, perhaps you had better go with me. I am bound to take you home again, if you do."

"There!" cried Diamond, who was still looking after the little girl. "I'm sure the wind will blow her over, and perhaps kill her. Do let me go."

They had been sweeping more slowly along the line of the street. There was a lull in the roaring.

"Well, though I cannot promise to take you home," said North Wind, as she sank nearer and nearer to the tops of the houses, "I can promise you it will be all right in the end. You will get home somehow. Have you made up your mind what to do?"

"Yes: to help the little girl," said Diamond firmly.

The same moment North Wind dropped into the street and stood, only a tall lady, but with her hair flying up over the housetops. She put her hands to her back, took Diamond, and set him down in the street. The same moment he was caught in the fierce coils of the blast, and all but blown away. North Wind stepped back a step, and at once towered in stature to the height of the houses. A chimney pot clashed at Diamond's feet. He turned to look for the little girl. When he turned back again the lady had vanished, and the wind was roaring along the street as if it had been an invisible torrent. The little girl was scudding before the blast, her hair flying too, and behind her she dragged her broom. Her little legs were going as fast as they could to keep her from falling. Diamond crept into the shelter of a doorway, thinking to stop her, but she passed him like a bird, crying gently and pitifully.

"Stop! Stop, little girl," shouted Diamond, starting in pursuit.

"I can't," wailed the girl, "the wind won't let go of me."

Diamond could run faster than she, and he had no broom. In a few moments he had caught her by the frock, but it tore in his hand, and away went the little girl. So he had to run again, and this time he ran so fast that he got in front of her, and turning around, caught her in his arms. Then down they both went together, which made the little girl laugh in the midst of her crying.

"Where are you going?" asked Diamond, rubbing the elbow that had stuck farthest out. The arm it belonged to was twined round a lamp post as he stood between the little girl and the wind.

"Home," she said, gasping for breath.

"Then I will go with you," said Diamond.

And then they were silent for a while, for the wind blew worse than ever, and they had to both hold on to the lamp post.

"Where is your crossing?" asked the girl at length.

"I don't sweep," answered Diamond.

"What do you do, then?" asked she. "You ain't big enough for most things."

"Nothing, I suppose. My father is Mr. Coleman's coachman."

"You have a father?" she said, staring at him as if a boy with a father was a natural curiosity.

"Yes. Haven't *you*?" returned Diamond.

"No; nor mother neither. Old Sal's all I've got." And she began to cry again.

"I wouldn't go to her if she wasn't good to me," said Diamond.

"But you must go somewheres," said the girl. "She'll laugh when she hears me crying at the door."

"You mean she won't let you in tonight?"

"I'll be lucky if she does."

"Why are you out so late, then?" asked Diamond.

"My crossing's a long way off at the West End, and I had been indulgin' in door steps and mewses."

"We'd better try anyhow," said Diamond. "Come along."

As he spoke Diamond thought he caught a glimpse of North Wind turning a corner in front of them; and when they turned the corner too, they found it quiet there, but he saw nothing of the lady.

"Now you lead me," he said, taking her hand, "and I'll take care of you."

The girl withdrew her hand, but only to dry her eyes with her frock, for the other had enough to do with her broom. She put it in his again, and led him, turning after turning, until they stopped at a cellar door in a very dirty lane. There she knocked.

"I shouldn't like to live here," said Diamond.

"Oh, yes, you would, if you had nowhere else to go to," answered the girl. "I only wish we could get in."

"I don't want to go in," said Diamond.

"Where do you plan to go, then?"

"Home to my home."

"Where's that?"

"I don't exactly know."

"Then you're worse off than I am."

"Oh no, for North Wind..." began Diamond, and stopped, he hardly knew why.

"What?" said the girl, as she held her ear to the door listening.

But Diamond did not reply. Neither did old Sal.

"I told you so," said the girl. "She is wide awake listening. But she won't let us in."

"What will you do, then?" asked Diamond.

"Move on," she answered.

"Where?"

"Oh, anywheres. Bless you, I'm used to it."

"Hadn't you better come home with me, then?"

"That's a good joke, when you don't know where it is. Come on."

"But where?" asked Diamond.

"Oh, nowheres in particular. Come on."

Diamond obeyed. The wind had now fallen considerably. They wandered on and on, turning in this direction and that, without any reason for one way more than another, until they had got out of the thick of the houses into a waste kind of place. By this time they were both very tired. Diamond felt a good deal inclined to cry, and thought he had been very silly to get down from the back of North Wind because he thought he had been of no use to the girl. He was mistaken there, because she was far happier for having Diamond with her than if she had been wandering about alone. She did not seem as tired as he was.

"I can't think how a kid like you comes to be out all alone this time o' night."

She called him a kid, but she was only a month older than he was, only she had had to work for her bread, and that so soon makes people older.

"But I shouldn't have been out so late if I hadn't got down to help you," said Diamond. "North Wind is gone home long ago."

"What are you talking about?" asked the girl. "You said something about the north wind afore that I couldn't get the rights of."

So now, for the sake of his character, Diamond had to tell her the whole story.

"I don't believe a word of it!" she said. But as she spoke there came a great blast of wind.

Diamond said, "Come on, let's keep going."

They wandered on and on, sometimes sitting on a door step, but always turning into lanes or fields when they had a chance.

They found themselves at last on a rising ground that sloped steeply on the other side. It was a waste kind of spot below, bounded by an irregular wall, with a few doors in it. Outside lay broken things in general, from garden rollers to flower pots and wine bottles. But the moment they reached the brow of the rising ground, a gust of wind seized them and blew them downhill as fast as they could run until they went bang against one of the doors in the wall. It burst open and they peeped in. It was the back door of a garden.

"Ah hah!" cried Diamond, after staring for a few moments. "I thought so! North Wind is true to her word! Here I am in master's garden! I tell you what, little girl, you just bore a hole in old Sal's wall, and put your mouth to it, and say, 'Please, North Wind, may I go out with you?' and then you'll see what'll come."

"But I'm out in the wind too often already to want more of it."

"I said with the North Wind, not in it."

"Good bye, mister," said the girl.

"Wait," he said. "Come in, and my mother will give you some breakfast."

"No, thank you. I must be off to my crossing. It's morning now."

"I'm very sorry for you," said Diamond.

"Well, it is a life to be tired of—what with old Sal, and so many holes in my shoes."

"I wonder you're so good. I should kill myself."

"Oh, no, you wouldn't! When I think of it, I always want to see what's coming next, and so I always wait till next is over. Well! I suppose there's somebody happy somewheres. But it ain't in them big carriages.
Oh my! How they do look sometimes—fit to bite your head off! Good bye!"

She ran up the hill and disappeared behind it. Then Diamond shut the door as best he could, and ran through the kitchen garden to the stable. And wasn't he glad to get into his own blessed bed again!

Diamond said nothing to his mother about his adventures. He had half a notion that North Wind was a friend of his mother, and that if she did not know all about it, at least she did not mind his going anywhere with the lady of the wind. At the same time he doubted whether he might not appear to be telling stories if he told all, especially as he could hardly believe it himself when he thought about it in the middle of the day, although when the twilight was once half way on to night he had no doubt about it, at least for the first few days after he had been with her. The girl that swept the crossing had certainly refused to believe him. Besides, he felt sure that North Wind would tell him if he ought to speak.

The summer drew near, warm and splendid. Miss Coleman was a little better in health, and sat a good deal in the garden. One day she saw Diamond peeping through the shrubbery, and called him. He talked to her so frankly that she often sent for him after that, and by degrees it came about that he had leave to run in the garden as he pleased. He never touched any of the flowers or blossoms, for he was not like some boys who cannot enjoy a thing without pulling it to pieces, and so preventing every one from enjoying it after them. Even a week makes such a long time in a child's life that Diamond had begun once more to feel as if North Wind were a dream of some far off year.

One hot evening, he had been sitting with the young mistress, as they called her, in a little summer house at the bottom of the lawn. It grew dusky, and the lady began to feel chill, and went in, leaving the boy in the summer house.

He sat there gazing out at a bed of tulips, which, although they had closed for the night, could not go quite asleep for the wind that kept waving them about. All at once he saw a great humble-bee fly out of one of the tulips.

"There! That is something done," said a voice—a gentle, merry, childish voice, but so tiny. "I thought he would have had to stay there all night, poor fellow!"

Diamond could not tell whether the voice was near or far away, it was so small and yet so clear. He had never seen a fairy, but he had heard of such, and he began to look all about for one. And there was the tiniest creature sliding down the stem of the tulip!

"Are you the fairy that herds the bees?" he asked, going out of the summer house, and down on his knees on the green shore of the tulip bed.

"I'm not a fairy," answered the little creature. "Diamond! Have you never seen me before?"

And, as she spoke, a moan of wind bent the tulips almost to the ground, and the creature laid her hand on Diamond's shoulder. In a moment he knew that it was North Wind.

"I never saw you so small before."

"Must you see me every size that can be measured before you know me, Diamond?"

"But how could I think it was you taking care of a great stupid bee?"

"The more stupid he was the more need he had to be taken care of.

"But how do you have time to look after bees?"

"I don't look after bees. I had this one to look after. It was hard work, though."

"Hard work! Why, you could blow a chimney down, or, or a boy's cap off," said Diamond.

"Both are easier than to blow a tulip open. But I scarcely know the difference between hard and easy. I am always able for what I have to do. When I see my work, I just rush at it, and it is done. But I mustn't chatter. I have got to sink a ship tonight."

"Sink a ship! What! With men in it?"

"Yes, and women too."

"How dreadful! I wish you wouldn't talk so."

"It is rather dreadful. But it is my work. I must do it."

"I hope you won't ask me to go with you."

"No, I won't ask you. But you must come for all that. It will be our last flight together for a while."

I don't want to. I won't.

"Won't you?" And North Wind grew a tall lady, and looked him in the eyes. Then Diamond said, "Please take me. You cannot be cruel."

"No. I could not be cruel if I would. I can do nothing cruel, although I often do what looks like cruel to those who do not know what I really am doing. The people they say I drown, I only carry away to...to... well, the back of the North Wind. That is what they used to call it long ago, only I never saw the place."

"How can you carry them there if you never saw it?"

"I know the way."

"But how is it you never saw it?"

"Because it is behind me."

"But you can look round."

"Not far enough to see my own back. No. I always look before me. In fact, I grow quite blind and deaf when I try to see my back. I only mind my work.

"But how does it become your work?"

"Ah, that I can't tell you.

I only know it is because when I do it I feel all right, and when I don't I feel all wrong. It is all one to me to let a bee out of a tulip, or to sweep the cobwebs from the sky. You would like to go with me tonight?"

"I don't want to see a ship sunk."

"But suppose I had to take you?"

"Why, then, of course I must go."

"There's a good Diamond. I think I had better be growing a bit. Only you must go to bed first. I can't take you till you're in bed. That's the law about the children. So I had better go and do something else first."

"Very well, North Wind," said Diamond. "What are you going to do first, if you please?"

"I think I may tell you. Jump up on the top of the wall."

"I can't."

"Ah! And I can't help you—you haven't been to bed yet, you see. Come out to the road with me, just in front of the coach house, and I will show you."

North Wind grew very small indeed, so small that she could not have blown the dust off a dusty miller, as the Scotch children call a yellow auricula. Diamond could not even see the blades of grass move as she flitted along by his foot. They left the lawn, went out by the wicket in the coach house gates, and then crossed the road to the low wall that separated it from the river.

"You can get up on this wall, Diamond," said North Wind.

"Yes, but my mother has forbidden me."

"Then don't," said North Wind.

"But I can see over," said Diamond.

"Ah! To be sure. I can't."

So saying, North Wind gave a little bound, and stood on the top of the wall. She was just about the height a dragonfly would be, if it stood on end.

"You darling!" said Diamond, seeing what a lovely little toy-woman she was.

"Don't be impertinent, Master Diamond," said North Wind. "If there's one thing makes me angry, it is the way you humans judge things by their size. I am quite as respectable now as I shall be six hours after this, when I take an East Indiaman by the royals, twist her round, and push her under. You have no right to address me in such a fashion."

But as she spoke, the tiny face wore the smile of a great, grand woman. She was only having her own beautiful fun out of Diamond, and true woman's fun never hurts.

"But look there!" she resumed. "Do you see a boat with one man in it—a green and white boat?"

"Yes, quite well."

"That's a poet."

"I thought you said it was a bo-at."

Don't you know what a poet is?"

"Why, a thing to sail on the water in."

"Well, perhaps you're not so far wrong. Some poets do carry people over the sea. But the man is a poet. A poet is a man who is glad of something, and tries to make other people glad of it too. But I see it is no use. I wasn't sent to tell you, and so I can't tell you. I must be off. Only first just look at the man."

"He's not much of a rower," said Diamond, "paddling first with one fin and then with the other."

"Now look here!" said North Wind.

And she flashed like a dragonfly across the water, whose surface rippled and puckered as she passed. The next moment the man in the boat glanced about him, and bent to his oars. The boat flew over the rippling water. Man and boat and river were awake. The same instant almost, North Wind perched again upon the river wall.

"How did you do that?" asked Diamond.

"I blew in his face," answered North Wind.

"I don't see how that could do it," said Diamond, "But I know you too well not to believe you."

"Well, I blew in his face, and that woke him up. Don't you see? Look at him, how he is pulling. I blew the mist out of him."

Diamond looked down to the wall. North Wind was gone. Away across the river went a long ripple—what sailors call a cat's paw. The man in the boat was adjusting the sail. The moon was coming to herself on the edge of a great cloud, and the sail began to shine white. Diamond rubbed his eyes, and wondered what it was all about. Things seemed going on around him, and all to understand each other, but he could make nothing of it. So he put his hands in his pockets, and went in to have his tea.

"You don't seem very well tonight, Diamond," said his mother.

"I think you had better go to bed," she added.

"Very well, mother," he answered.

He stopped for one moment to look out of the window. Above the moon the clouds were going different ways. Somehow or other this troubled him, but, notwithstanding, he was soon fast asleep.

He woke in the middle of the night and the darkness. A terrible noise was rumbling overhead, like the rolling beat of great drums echoing through a brazen vault. The roof of the loft in which he lay had no ceiling; only the tiles were between him and the sky. For a while he could not come quite awake, for the noise kept beating him down, so that his heart was troubled and fluttered painfully. A second peal of thunder burst over his head, and almost choked him with fear. Nor did he recover until the great blast that followed, having torn some tiles off the roof, sent a spout of wind down into his bed and over his face, which brought him wide awake, and gave him back his courage. The same moment he heard a mighty yet musical voice calling him.

"Come up, Diamond," it said. "It's all ready. I'm waiting for you."

He looked out of the bed, and saw a gigantic, powerful, but most lovely arm—with a hand whose fingers were nothing the less ladylike that they could have strangled a boa constrictor, or choked a tigress off its prey—stretched down through a big hole in the roof. Without a moment's hesitation he reached out his tiny one, and laid it in the grand palm before him.

The hand felt its way up his arm, and, grasping it gently and strongly above the elbow, lifted Diamond from the bed. The moment he was through the hole in the roof, all the winds of heaven seemed to lay hold of him, and buffet him here and there. His hair blew one way, his nightshirt another, his legs threatened to float from under him, and his head to grow dizzy with the swiftness of the invisible assailant. Cowering, he clung with the other hand to the huge hand which held his arm, and fear invaded his heart.

"Oh, North Wind!" he murmured, but the words vanished from his lips, the wind caught them, and they were nowhere. And yet North Wind heard them, and in her answer it seemed that because she was so big and could not help it, and because her ear and her mouth must seem to him so dreadfully far away, she spoke to him more tenderly and graciously than ever before. Her voice was like the bass of a deep organ, without the groan in it; like the most delicate of violin tones without the wail in it; like the sound of falling water without the clatter and clash in it: it was like all of them and none of them—all of them without their faults, each of them without its peculiarity. And after all, it was more like his mother's voice than anything else in the world.

"Diamond, dear," she said, "what is fearful to you is not at all fearful to me."

"But it can't hurt you," murmured Diamond, "for you're it."

"Then if I'm it, and have you in my arms, how can it hurt you?"

"Oh yes! I see," whispered Diamond. "But it looks so dreadful, and it pushes me about so much."

"Yes, it does, my dear. That is what it was sent for."

At the same moment, a peal of thunder which shook Diamond's heart against the sides of his rib cage hurtled out of the heavens: I cannot say out of the sky, for there was no sky.

"Diamond, dear, this will never do."

"Oh yes, it will," answered Diamond. "I am all right now—quite comfortable, I assure you, dear North Wind. If you will only let me stay here, I shall be all right indeed."

"But you will feel the wind here, Diamond."

"I don't mind that a bit, so long as I feel your arms through it," answered Diamond, nestling closer to her.

"Brave boy!" returned North Wind, pressing him closer.

"No," said Diamond, "I don't see that. It's not courage at all, so long as I feel you there."

"But hadn't you better get into my hair? Then you would not feel the wind; you will here."

"Ah, but, dear North Wind, you don't know how nice it is to feel your arms about me. It is a thousand times better to have them and the wind together, than to have only your hair and the back of your neck and no wind at all."

"But it is surely more comfortable there?"

"Well, perhaps; but I begin to think there are better things than being comfortable."

"Yes, indeed there are. Well, I will keep you in front of me. You will feel the wind, but not too much. I shall only want one arm to take care of you. The other will be quite enough to sink the ship."

"Oh, dear North Wind! How can you talk so?"

"My dear boy, I always mean what I say."

"Then you do mean to sink the ship with the other hand?"

"Yes."

"It's not like you."

"How do you know that?"

"Quite easily. Here you are taking care of a poor little boy with one arm, and there you are sinking a ship with the other. It can't be like you."

"Ah! But which is me? I can't be two mes, you know."

"No. Nobody can be two mes."

"Well, which me is me?"

"Now I must think. There appears to be two."

"Yes. That's the very point. You can't be sure of the thing you don't know, can you?"

"No."

"Which me do you know?"

"The kindest, best you in the world," answered Diamond, clinging to North Wind.

"Why am I good to you?"

"I don't know, except because it's good to be good to me."

"That's just it. I am good to you because I like to be good."

"Then why shouldn't you be good to other people as well as to me?"

"Well,
but I am."

"There it is again," said
Diamond. "I don't see that you are.
It looks quite the opposite."

"Listen to me, Diamond. You know the one me, you say, who is
good. Do you know the other me as well?"

"No. I can't. I don't want to."

"There. You don't know the other me. You are sure of one of them?
And you are sure there can't be two of me?"

"Yes."

"Then the me you don't know must be the same as the me you do know, otherwise there
would be two of me?"

"Yes."

"Then the me you don't know must be as kind as the me you do know?"

"Yes."

"Besides, I tell you that it is true. It only doesn't appear so. That I confess freely. Have you anything more to
object to?"

"No, no, dear North Wind; I am quite satisfied. You may sink as many ships as you like, and I won't say
another word. But I can't say I shall like to see it, you know."

"That's quite another thing," said North Wind; and as she spoke she gave one spring from the roof of the
hay loft, and rushed up into the clouds, with Diamond on her arm, close to her heart. And as if the clouds
knew she had come, they burst into a fresh jubilation of thunderous light. For a few moments, Diamond
seemed to be borne up through the depths of an ocean of dazzling flame; the next, the winds were writhing
around him like a storm of serpents. Now it blinded him by smiting him upon the eyes; now it deafened him
by bellowing in his ears. But he did not mind. He only gasped first and then laughed, for the arm of North
Wind was about him, and he was leaning against her. It is quite impossible for me to describe what he saw.
Did you ever watch a great wave shoot into a winding passage among rocks? If you ever did, you would see
that the water rushed every way at once, some of it even turning back and opposing the rest; you might see
greater confusion nowhere else except in a crowd of frightened people. Well, the wind was like that, except

that it went much faster, and therefore was much wilder, and twisted and shot and curled and dodged and clashed and raved ten times more madly than anything else in creation except human passions. Diamond saw the threads of the lady's hair streaking it all. Sometimes he could not tell which was hair and which was black storm and vapor. It also seemed to Diamond that they were motionless in this center, and that all the confusion and fighting went on around them. Flash after flash illuminated the fierce chaos; peal after peal of thunder tore the infinite waste. But it seemed to Diamond that North Wind and he were motionless, all but the hair. It was not so. They were sweeping with the speed of the wind itself towards the sea.

Before they reached the sea, Diamond felt North Wind's hair just beginning to fall about him.

"Is the storm over, North Wind?" he called out.

"No, Diamond. I am only waiting a moment to put you down. You would not like to see the ship sunk, so I am going to give you a place to wait till I come back for you."

"Oh! Thank you," said Diamond. "I shall be sorry to leave you, North Wind, but I would rather not see the ship go down. And I'm afraid the poor people will cry, and I should hear them. Oh, dear!"

"There are a good many passengers on board; and to tell the truth, Diamond, I don't want you to hear this cry you speak of."

"But how can you bear it then, North Wind? For I am sure you are kind. I shall never doubt that again."

"I will tell you how I am able to bear it, Diamond: I am always hearing, through every noise, even through all the noise I am making myself, the sound of a far off song. I do not exactly know where it is, or what it means, and I don't hear much of it, only the odor of its music, as it were, flitting across the great billows of the ocean outside this storm. But what I do hear is quite enough to make me able to bear the cry from the drowning ship. So it would be for you if you could hear it."

"No, it wouldn't," returned Diamond, stoutly. "For they wouldn't hear the music of the far-away song; and if they did, it wouldn't do them any good. You see you and I are not going to be drowned, and so we might enjoy it."

"But you have never heard the psalm, and you don't know what it is like. Somehow, I can't say how, it tells me that all is right; that it is coming, to swallow up all cries."

"But that won't do them any good—the people, I mean," persisted Diamond.

"It must. It must," said North Wind, hurriedly. "It wouldn't be the song it seems to be if it did not swallow up all their fear and pain too, and set them singing it themselves with the rest. I am sure it will. And do you know, ever since I knew I had hair, that is, ever since it began to go out and away, that song has been coming nearer and nearer. But it was a thousand years before I heard it."

"But how can you say it was coming nearer when you did not hear it?" asked doubting little Diamond.

"Since I first heard it, I have known that it is growing louder, therefore I judge that it has been coming nearer and nearer until I first heard it. I'm not so very old, you know—a few thousand years only—and I was quite a baby when I heard the noise first, but I knew it must come from the voices of people ever so much older and wiser than I was.

Now. Will you wait here?"

"I can't see anywhere to wait," said Diamond. "Your hair is all down like a darkness, and I can't see through."

"Look, then," said North Wind; and, with one sweep of her great white arm, she swept yards deep of darkness like a great curtain from before the face of the boy.

And lo! It was a blue night, lit up with stars. Where it did not shine with stars it shimmered with the milk of the stars, except where, just opposite to Diamond's face, the grey towers of a cathedral loomed.

"Oh! What's that?" cried Diamond, struck with a kind of terror, for he had never seen a cathedral, and it rose before him with an awful reality in the midst of the wide spaces, conquering emptiness with grandeur.

"A very good place for you to wait in," said North Wind. "But we shall go in, and you shall judge for yourself."

There was an open door in the middle of one of the towers, leading out upon the roof, and through it they passed. Then North Wind set Diamond on his feet, and he found himself at the top of a stone stair, which went twisting away down into the darkness for only a little light came in at the door. It was enough, however, to allow Diamond to see that North Wind stood beside him. He looked up to find her face, and saw that she was no longer a beautiful giantess, but the tall gracious lady he liked best to see. She took his hand, and, giving him the broad part of the spiral stair to walk on, led him down a good way.

Then, opening another little door, she led him out upon a narrow gallery that ran all round the ledges of the windows. It was very narrow, and Diamond saw nothing to keep him from falling into the church. It lay below him like a great silent gulf hollowed in stone, and he held his breath for fear as he looked down.

"What are you trembling for, little Diamond?" said the lady, as she walked gently along, with her hand held out behind her leading him, for there was not breadth enough for them to walk side by side.

"I am afraid of falling down there," answered Diamond. "It is so deep down."

"Yes, rather," answered North Wind. "But you were a hundred times higher a few minutes ago."

"Ah, yes, but your arm was about me then," said Diamond.

Don't you know I have a hold of you?"

"Yes, but I'm walking on my own legs, and they might slip. I can't trust myself so well as your arms."

"But I have a hold of you, I tell you, child."

"Yes, but somehow I can't feel comfortable."

"If you were to fall, and my hold of you were to give way, I should be down after you in a less moment than a lady's watch can tick, and catch you long before you had reached the ground."

"I don't like it though," said Diamond.

"Oh! oh! oh!" he screamed the next moment, bent double with terror, for North Wind had let go her hold of his hand, and had vanished, leaving him standing as if rooted to the gallery.

She left the words, "Come after me," sounding in his ears.

But move he dared not. In a moment more he would from very terror have fallen into the church, but suddenly there came a gentle breath of cool wind upon his face, and it kept blowing upon him in little puffs, and at every puff Diamond felt his faintness going away, and his fear with it. Courage was reviving in his little heart, and still the cool wafts of the soft wind breathed upon him, and the soft wind was so mighty and strong within its gentleness, that in a minute more Diamond was marching along the narrow ledge, as fearless for the time, as North Wind herself.

He walked on and on, with the windows all in a row on one side of him, and the great empty nave of the church echoing to every one of his brave strides on the other. At last he came to a little open door, from which a broader stair led him down and down, till all at once he found himself in the arms of North Wind, who held him close to her, and kissed him on the forehead. Diamond nestled into her, and murmured, "Why did you leave me, dear North Wind?"

"Because I wanted you to walk alone," she answered.

"But it is so much nicer here!" said Diamond.

"I daresay. But I couldn't hold a little coward to my heart. It would make me so cold!"

"But I wasn't brave of myself," said Diamond, whom my older readers will have already discovered to be a true child in this, that he was given to metaphysics. "It was the wind that blew in my face that made me brave. Wasn't it now, North Wind?"

"Yes. I know that. You had to be taught what courage was. And you couldn't know what it was without feeling it: therefore it was given to you. But don't you feel as if you would try to be brave yourself next time?"

"Yes, I do. But trying is not much."

"Yes, it is—a very great deal, for it is a beginning. And a beginning is the greatest thing of all. To try to be brave is to be brave. The coward who tries to be brave is ahead of the man who is brave because he is made so, and never had to try."

"How kind you are, North Wind!"

"I am only just. All kindness is but justice. We owe it."

"I don't quite understand that."

"Never mind. You will someday. There is no hurry about understanding it now."

"Who blew the wind on me that made me brave?"

"I did."

"I didn't see you."

"Therefore you can believe me."

"But how was it that such a little breath could be so strong?"

"That I don't know."

"But you made it strong?"

"No: I only blew it. I knew it would make you strong, just as it did the man in the boat, you remember. But how my breath has that power I cannot tell. It was put into it when I was made. That is all I know. But really I must be going about my work."

"Ah! The poor ship! I wish you would stay here, and let the poor ship go."

"That I dare not do. Wait here until I come back."

"Yes. You won't be long?"

"Not longer than I can help. Trust me, you shall get home before the morning."

In a moment North Wind was gone, and the next Diamond heard a moaning about the church, which grew and grew to a roaring. The storm was up again, and he knew that North Wind's hair was flying.

The church was dark and grew very lonely about him, and he began to feel like a child whose mother has forsaken it. Only he knew that to be left alone is not always to be forsaken.

He began to feel his way about the place, and for a while went wandering up and down. His little footsteps waked little answering echoes in the great house It was as if the church knew he was there, and meant to make itself his house. So it went on giving back an answer to every step, until at length Diamond thought he should like to say something out loud, and see what the church would answer. But he found he was afraid to speak. He could not utter a word for fear of the loneliness. Perhaps it was as well that he did not, for the sound of a spoken word would have made him feel the place yet more deserted and empty. But he thought he could sing. He was fond of singing, and at home he used to sing, to tunes of his own, all the nursery rhymes he knew. So he began to try a few, but they just wouldn't do. They all sounded so silly, although he had never thought them silly before. So he was quiet, and listened to the echoes that came out of the dark corners in answer to his footsteps.

At last he gave a great sigh, and said, "I'm so tired." But he did not hear the gentle echo that answered from far away over his head, for at the same moment he came against the lowest of a few steps that stretched across the church. At the top he came to a little bit of carpet, on which he lay down; and there he lay staring at the dull window that rose nearly a hundred feet above his head.

Now this was the eastern window of the church, and the moon was at that moment just on the edge of the horizon. The next, she was peeping over it. And lo! With the moon, St. John and St. Paul, and the rest of them, began to dawn in the window in their lovely garments. Diamond did not know that the wonder-working moon was behind, and he thought all the light was coming out of the window itself, and that the good old men were appearing to help him, growing out of the night and the darkness, because he was very tired and lonely, and North Wind was so long in coming. So he lay and looked at them backwards over his head, wondering when they would come down or what they would do next. They were very dim, for the moonlight was not strong enough for the colors. So his eyes grew tired, and his eyelids grew so heavy that they would keep tumbling down over his eyes. He kept lifting them but every time they were heavier than the last. At length he gave up, and the moment he gave up, he was fast asleep.

That Diamond had fallen fast asleep is very evident from the strange things he now fancied as taking place. For he thought he heard a sound as of whispering up in the great window. He tried to open his eyes, but he could not. And the whispering went on and grew louder and louder, until he could hear every word that was said. He thought it was the Apostles talking about him. But he could not open his eyes.

"And how comes he to be lying there, St. Peter?" said one.

"I think I saw him a while ago up in the gallery, under the Nicodemus window. Perhaps he has fallen down. What do you think, St. Matthew?"

"I don't think he could have crept here after falling from such a height. He must have been killed."

"What are we to do with him? We can't leave him lying there. And we could not make him comfortable up here in the window: it's rather crowded already. What do you say, St. Thomas?"

"Let's go down and look at him."

There came a rustling, and a chinking, and then there was a silence for some time, and Diamond felt somehow that all the Apostles were standing round him and looking down on him. And still he could not open his eyes.

"What is the matter with him, St. Luke?" asked one.

"There's nothing the matter with him," answered St. Luke, who must have joined the company of the Apostles from the next window, one would think. "He's in a sound sleep."

"I have it," cried another. "This is one of North Wind's tricks. She has caught him up and dropped him at our door, like a withered leaf or a foundling baby. I don't understand that woman's conduct, I must say. As if we hadn't enough to do with our money, without going taking care of other people's children! That's not what our forefathers built cathedrals for."

Now Diamond could not bear to hear such things against North Wind, who, he knew, never played anybody a trick. She was far too busy with her own work for that. He struggled hard to open his eyes, but without success.

"She should consider that a church is not a place for pranks, not to mention that we live in it," said another.

"It certainly is disrespectful of her. But she always is disrespectful. What right has she to bang at our windows as she has been doing the whole of this night? I daresay there is glass broken somewhere. I know my blue robe is in a dreadful mess with the rain first and the dust after. It will cost me shillings to clean it."

Then Diamond knew that they could not be Apostles, talking like this. They could only be the sextons and vergers and such-like, who got up at night, and put on the robes of deans and bishops, and called each other grand names, as the foolish servants he had heard his father tell of call themselves lords and ladies, after their masters and mistresses. And he was so angry at their daring to abuse North Wind, that he jumped up, crying, "North Wind knows best what she is about. She has a good right to blow the cobwebs from your windows, for she was sent to do it. She sweeps them away from grander places, I can tell you, for I've been with her at it."

This was what he began to say, but as he spoke his eyes came wide open, and behold, there were neither Apostles nor vergers there—not even a window with the effigies of holy men in it, but a dark heap of hay all about him, and the little panes in the roof of his loft glimmering blue in the light of the morning.

Old Diamond was coming awake down below in the stable. In a moment more he was on his feet, and shaking himself so that young Diamond's bed trembled under him.

He got up and dressed himself. Then he went out into the garden. There must have been a tremendous wind in the night, for although all was quiet now, there lay the little summer house crushed to the ground, and over it the great elm tree, which the wind had broken across, being much decayed in the middle. Diamond almost cried to see the wilderness of green leaves, which used to be so far up in the blue air, tossing about in the breeze, now lying so near the ground, and without any hope of ever getting up into the deep air again.

"I wonder how old the tree is!" thought Diamond. "It must take a long time to get so near the sky as that poor tree was."

"Yes, indeed," said a voice beside him, for Diamond had spoken the last words aloud.

Diamond started, and looking around saw a clergyman, a brother of Mrs. Coleman, who happened to be visiting her. He was a great scholar, and was in the habit of rising early.

"Who are you, my man?" he added.

"Little Diamond," answered the boy.

"Oh! I have heard of you. How do you come to be up so early?"

"Because the sham Apostles talked such nonsense, they waked me up."

The clergyman stared. Diamond saw that he had better have held his tongue, for he could not explain things.

"You must have been dreaming, my little man," said he. "Dear! dear!" he went on, looking at the tree, "there has been terrible work here. This is the north wind's doing. What a pity! I wish we lived at the back of it, I'm sure."

"Where is that, sir?" asked Diamond.

"Away in the Hyperborean regions," answered the clergyman, smiling.

"I never heard of the place," returned Diamond.

"I daresay not," answered the clergyman, "but if this tree had been there now, it would not have been blown down, for there is no wind there."

"But, please, sir, if it had been there," said Diamond, "we should not have had to be sorry for it."

"Certainly not."

"Then we shouldn't have had to be glad for it, either."

"You're quite right, my boy," said the clergyman, looking at him very kindly, as he turned away to the house, with his eyes bent towards the earth.

But Diamond thought within himself, "I will ask North Wind next time I see her to take me to that country. I think she did speak about it once before."

And this is just what Diamond did.

But that part of the story is for another book.

George MacDonald
1824-1905

George MacDonald was a Scottish author, poet and minister who wrote over 50 volumes of novels, poems, essays, and fairy tales. He was one of the most beloved writers of the 19th century, both in the U.K. and in America. Most well-known among the fairy tales are *The Princess and the Goblin*, *The Light Princess*, and *At the Back of the North Wind*. Regarding his stories, MacDonald wrote: "For my part, I do not write for children, but for the childlike, whether of 5, or 50, or 75."

Friends and colleagues included John Ruskin, Walt Whitman, Mark Twain and Lewis Carroll. Many writers were greatly influenced by him, including J.R.R. Tolkien, G.K. Chesterton, Madeleine L'Engle and C.S. Lewis.

Madeleine L'Engle called George MacDonald "the grandfather of us all—all of us who struggle to come to terms with truth through imagination."

C.S. Lewis wrote: "I have never concealed the fact that I regarded him as my master, indeed I fancy I have never written a book in which I did not quote from him."
—preface to *George MacDonald: An Anthology*

At the Back of the North Wind

Illustrator's Note

At The Back of the North Wind was first published in serialized form in 1861 for the children's magazine, *Good Words for the Young*. It included 38 chapters and unfolded gradually over two years. It was published in book form in 1871.

In presenting this excerpt, I hope to introduce more people to this wonderful tale. I tried to keep intact as much of the original language as possible; MacDonald's voice is uniquely beautiful and well worth experiencing. Because the full version was originally written as a serial story, I thought it might be daunting for a new reader to tackle a 350-page volume. It includes many wonderful poems and even a story within the story. But I feel that as an introduction, this first section, *Diamond and the North Wind*, is a beautiful stand-alone tale, that I hope will entice readers to further explore George MacDonald's writings. The full North Wind story is rich and well worth reading, as are all of his other fairy tales and fables.

He once wrote, "The best thing you can do for your fellow, next to rousing his conscience, is, not to give him things to think about, but to wake things up that are in him, or say, to make him think things for himself...If there be music in my reader, I would gladly wake it..."
"If any strain of my 'broken music' make a child's eye flash, or his mother's grow for a moment dim, my labour will not have been in vain."
–George MacDonald, *The Fantastic Imagination*

—JW